HarperCollins®, 📖®, and HarperKidsEntertainment™
are trademarks of HarperCollins Publishers.

Open Season: The Movie Storybook
™ & © 2006 Sony Pictures Animation, Inc. All rights reserved.
Printed in the United States of America.
For information address HarperCollins Children's Books, a division of HarperCollins Publishers,
1350 Avenue of the Americas, New York, NY 10019.
www.harpercollinschildrens.com
Library of Congress catalog card number: 2006926600
ISBN-10: 0-06-084609-7—ISBN-13: 978-0-06-084609-1
Book design by John Sazaklis ❖

First Edition

OPEN SEASON

The Movie Storybook

Adapted by Kate Egan

HarperKidsEntertainment
An Imprint of HarperCollinsPublishers

Boog was not your typical gigantic grizzly bear. While he did have huge teeth, sharp claws, and a monstrous roar, he was a sweet, friendly fuzz ball with a heart of gold.

Boog didn't live in the forest—he'd never even been there! Instead, he lived with a park ranger named Beth. He slept in her garage, in a bed of his own. He even had a teddy bear named Dinkelman! Boog was spoiled rotten.

Beth's house was in a tiny town named Timberline, nestled in the Sawtooth Mountains. Its scenery was majestic, with craggy peaks and sweeping vistas, but Timberline's Main Street was sleepy, and visitors never stayed too long in town . . . unless it was hunting season. Then people poured into Timberline from far and wide.

Beth put on a daily show for the various visitors with the help of Boog at the local amphitheater. "I'm Ranger Beth," she began cheerfully. "Today, we're going to meet North America's largest omnivore. Behold, the mighty grizzly!"

Behind a curtain, Boog had been waiting for this cue. He rode a unicycle onstage and roared at the top of his lungs! The audience clapped and cheered. Boog was happy and safe—and the star attraction.

After the show was over, Beth walked Boog to her jeep and told him to wait outside as she went into the Fish and Game office. Shaw, the meanest hunter around, had parked his jeep right next to Boog. The bear noticed a deer tied to the hood of Shaw's truck.

Boog poked the deer with a stick . . . then suddenly the deer's eyes popped open!

"Where am I? Am I dead?" asked the deer.

"Not yet," said Boog. "But seeing as how that's Shaw's truck . . ."

"What's a Shaw?" the deer asked nervously.

"Only the nastiest hunter in town," Boog told him.

When the deer asked Boog to untie him, Boog shook his head. He felt sorry for the deer, but he didn't want to get involved.

"What am I gonna do?" the deer wailed. "I don't want to be mounted on a wall!"

That wasn't about to happen. One of his antlers was missing! Boog swiveled Shaw's rearview mirror so the deer could see.

"Aaaaauuuggghhh!" screeched the deer. "Don't look at me! I'm hideous!"

Just then, Beth arrived. "Boog, come on, let's get out of here," she said angrily.

The deer wouldn't leave Boog alone. "Come on! I'm begging you!" he whispered.

Boog couldn't take it anymore. With one swish of his claw, he untied the deer's ropes.

From the window of the Fish and Game office, Shaw could see what was happening. "My buck!" Shaw screamed. But before he could do anything, the deer, the bear, and Beth were gone.

That night, Beth tucked Boog into his warm bed. Beth gave the bear an extra fishy cracker after he flashed her his famous grin.

Beth always gave in to Boog when he smiled at her that way.

Boog snuggled up and fell fast asleep . . . until he heard something crash into his window.

"Who's there?" he growled. "I got ten claws and I ain't afraid to use 'em!"

Suddenly the garage window opened and the deer fell in!

"Hey, buddy! It's me, Elliot!" the deer yelled.

"What are you doing here?" asked Boog.

"You helped me," said Elliot. "I'm returning the favor. I'm bustin' you out of here!"

Boog shook his head. He didn't need the deer's help. "This here is my home!" he said proudly.

"Sweet," whistled Elliot slowly, taking it all in. "I get it. You're like a pet!"

Boog didn't like the way that sounded. "I do what I want!" he exclaimed.

"Well then, let's go!" said Elliot.

The grizzly had his doubts. But Elliot was eating something, and Boog's nose kept drawing him toward it!

"What's that?" Boog asked.

"I call 'em Woo-Hoos. You want one?" Elliot asked. Boog sniffed at the candy bar as Elliot waved it back and forth.

"I know where there's a bunch more of them, but you gotta go outside," said Elliot. Boog hesitated for a minute, but the thought of more Woo-Hoo bars convinced him to follow Elliot.

Elliot led them right to the PuniMart convenience store. Boog struggled to open the door, but it was locked.

Elliot wasn't so timid. He crashed a shopping cart right through the PuniMart's front door!

Boog scooped up an armful of candy bars and swallowed them all at once, wrapper and all. He and Elliot ran wild through the store, gobbling chips and pizza, hot dogs and bubble gum. It was the most fun Boog had ever had . . . until Elliot noticed the flashing police lights. The deer ran out the back door, but Boog was in a state of sugar shock and didn't get out in time. Sheriff Gordy hauled him home in disgrace.

"You're in big trouble, mister," Beth said. "You know what sugar does to you, Boog. Straight to bed!"

As Boog stumbled toward the garage, Beth spoke to Sheriff Gordy. "It's all my fault. It won't happen again," she apologized.

But Gordy wanted her to return Boog to the wild! "Beth, you're not his mother," he said gently. "The longer you wait, the harder it's going to be for him to adapt. And the harder it's going to be for you to let him go."

Beth knew he was right, but she wasn't ready to face it.

Elliot hid from the police all night. But the next day he ran up against something much worse. . . . Shaw, the hunter.

Shaw hadn't forgotten the way Boog freed his deer. He'd seen the animals working together, and he wasn't going to let it happen again. Shaw chased Elliot all over town until the deer crashed into the amphitheater where Boog's show was about to begin!

"Hide me!" Elliot begged.

"You got me in enough trouble already!" said Boog. "Get out!" Boog was angry and he chased Elliot around backstage.

The audience couldn't hear the animals arguing. But it could see their shadows on the curtain—and it looked like Boog was about to kill a deer! The crowd panicked and ran up the aisles and out of the theater.

Shaw was standing by, ready to capture Boog and Elliot. Beth beat him to it, tranquilizing both animals with darts.

Boog had never acted like this before. She wondered what had gotten into her bear.

"It's time, Beth," Gordy said when he appeared on the scene.

"But hunting season begins in three days!" she reminded him. There couldn't be a worse time to release Boog into the wild.

Gordy insisted that Beth take Boog above the falls. The bear would be safe there.

Later that day, Beth landed her helicopter high in the mountains and untied the big sack that held her sleeping bear, his teddy bear, and the deer. "I'm going to miss you, big guy," she said tenderly. She gave him one last hug, then took off into the sunset.

Boog *was* fine when he woke up . . . until he realized he was in a meadow
full of chirping birds and chattering squirrels.

"Where's home?" he sputtered. "It's gone! Someone stole it!"

Suddenly Elliot's head popped out of the sack, too. Boog glared at him.
"My life is missing," he fumed. "And it's all your fault." Boog threw Elliot over
his shoulder, and the deer landed headfirst, his antler stuck in the ground.

Boog was desperate to get back home and was about to take off into the forest,
but he realized he had no clue where he was going.

Finally Elliot piped up. "Boog! Wait! I know where Timberline is. I can get

Boog thought if he could climb high enough, he could get the lay of the land.
He was halfway to the top of a tree when a strange voice growled, "Oi! Lost your
way, pal? This is McSquizzy's turf!"

Even Boog wasn't scared of a squirrel, until about a hundred more of them
appeared in the branches above him. "Mess not with the Furry Tail Clan," declared
McSquizzy.

Wisely, Boog deserted the tree and chose another—only to get bonked in the head
with an acorn! All the trees belonged to the squirrels!

Embarrassed, Boog found his way back to Elliot. He plucked the deer out of the ground and demanded directions back to town.

"I'll take you to town, but when we get there we're partners," Elliot said. "Deal? Partners."

"Forget it," grumbled Boog. He couldn't believe this guy.

"Better start moving then," Elliot announced, "'Cause open season starts in a few days. Maybe one of those hunters can give you a ride on the hood of his truck!"

Boog hadn't thought about hunters. They could definitely keep him from getting back to where he belonged—and he didn't stand a chance against them alone.

Reluctantly, Boog put his paw in Elliot's hoof and shook. "Partners," he muttered.

"Okeydokey!" rejoiced Elliot. "This way! Move it or lose it!"

Elliot kept talking as they made their way into the forest. "You know, I was think-ing we should have a secret handshake and, like, cool nicknames. I'll call you 'Boogster' and you can call me 'The Incredible Mr. E.'"

Behind him, the grizzly bear rolled his eyes. It was hard to believe that being stuck with Elliot was better than being left to the hunters. But if he wanted to get home, he'd have to stick with the deer.

He followed Elliot up a cliff, but his arms wobbled and, next thing he knew, he was hanging over the cliff by one paw! "Elliot!" he called out, frightened.

Then Boog lost his grip, cartwheeled down the mountainside, and crashed into a tree. He fell off a branch and landed squarely on a porcupine!

Boog squeezed his eyes shut when Elliot ripped the porcupine off. The porcupine gazed gratefully at Elliot as the bigger animals moved away.

After a while, they passed a bunch of beavers on a break from building a dam.
Elliot saw that the beavers couldn't take their eyes off the largest omnivore in
America—Boog. Elliot couldn't help but comment, "And he's a good dancer, too.
We're gonna be in a show!"

Right in front of the beavers, Boog exploded. "Listen, we are not *we*! And we ain't
doing no show."

Elliot suggested eating something and handed him a pinecone. "I can't eat that!"
Boog cried.

"Picky, picky, picky," said Elliot. "Well, what do bears eat?"

Boog thought for a minute. "Mmm. Ah. Fish!" But he couldn't manage to catch a
salmon, no matter how long he waited on the riverbank. The water sparkled in the
sunlight, but Boog didn't notice. He was too miserable.

Boog felt like a total failure as a bear—and that was before nature called.

"Uh, hey, Incredible Mr. E," he began.

"Yeeeesss, Boogster?" Elliot asked.

"I gotta go," said Boog.

"Well, go," said Elliot. He didn't know what Boog was getting at.

"No, I need a toilet," Boog snapped impatiently. But of course he was going to have to do what other animals did. So Boog squatted over a bush, and suddenly he had an audience: squirrels and the porcupine, rabbits, and even skunks! The bush belonged to two skunks named Rosie and Maria, and they didn't like Boog sitting on their home. So they sprayed him in the face!

"The woods are no place for a bear," Boog mumbled.

While Boog ran to the riverbank to clean up, Elliot spotted a pretty doe he knew and tried to replace his missing antler with a tree branch. "Pssst! Giselle!" he whispered when he was looking his best.

Suddenly the two of them were surrounded by a herd of deer.

"Hello, Smelliot," smirked a huge deer. Ian was the leader of the herd— and Giselle's boyfriend. "You've got a lot of nerve. I told you to leave the herd and never ever come back!"

Ian slammed his front hooves into Elliot, and he went flying.

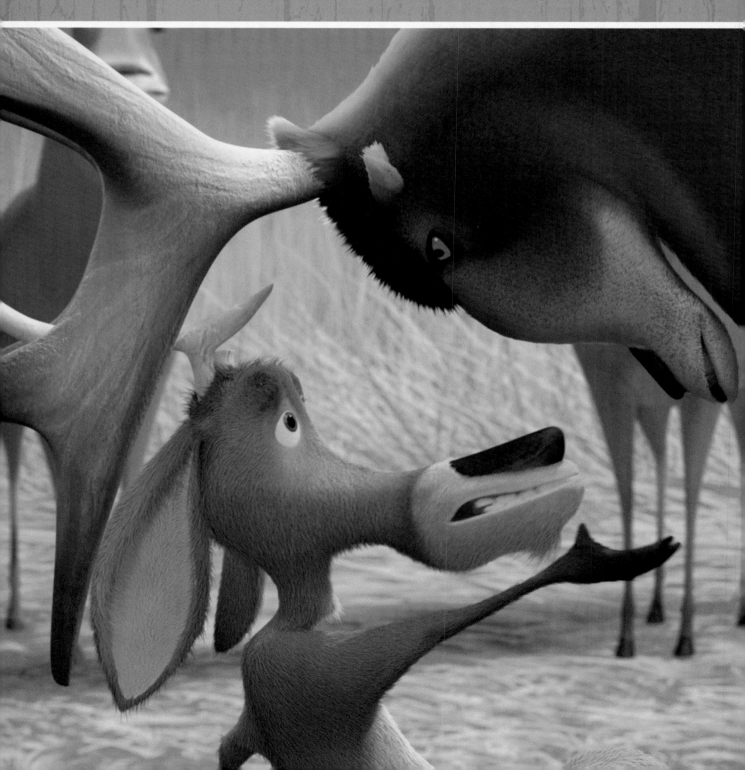

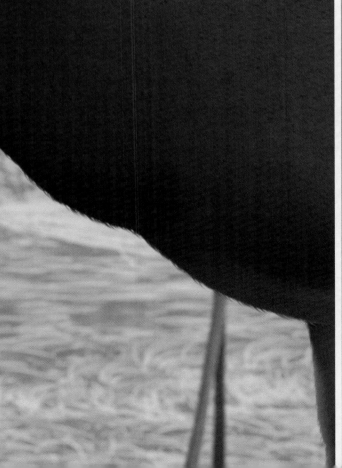

Overhearing Elliot's scream, Boog came running.

He charged into the circle of deer and asked "Elliot, are you all right?" For a moment Ian thought there was a dangerous grizzly on the scene, but then he saw Boog's teddy bear!

Ian figured Boog out pretty fast, and soon he was teasing him the way he'd teased Elliot. "Boog, let's go," Elliot said, dragging him away.

Ian mocked them as they walked off. "You two are perfect for each other," he yelled, looking from one to the other. "You're a loser, and you're a loser-er!"

That evening, Boog and Elliot plopped into the grass, exhausted. "Ian's right," Elliot said sadly. "I *am* a loser. First he kicked me out of the herd. Then I lost my antler, and then I got run over. What do you call that?"

"A loser," Boog admitted. "But, check this out. I can't fish, I can't climb a tree, I can't even go in the woods!"

"At least you've got a home," Elliot pointed out. It was a lot more than he had.

"Oh . . . uh . . . when we get back home tomorrow . . . maybe we can find a place for you in the garage," Boog replied.

"Sweet!" Elliot exclaimed. He had made a friend, and now he was going to have a home!

Meanwhile, two campers, Bob and Bobbie, were toasting marshmallows over a fire. Their tiny dog, Mr. Weenie, was watching intently—but the campers weren't sharing their treats.

"Come on, Mr. Weenie!" Bobbie said. "Beg! You can do it!" Bob got down on all fours to demonstrate.

Deep in the woods, Shaw was watching—and he couldn't believe his eyes! A human was begging a dog for food! What was next? Dogs walking humans? Animals taking over the world? The hunter knew what he had seen and he knew the animals had to be stopped!

The next morning, Boog and Elliot hiked through the forest, around trees, and through tall grass.

Boog was starting to feel more comfortable. Was he adjusting to life in the wild? *Or had he seen it all before?*

Boog grabbed Elliot by the throat and hissed "We've been going in circles!" Maybe he couldn't trust Elliot after all.

Suddenly, a shot rang out through the clear blue sky. Boog knew it was hunting season—but somehow he hadn't expected this.

Elliot's voice was shaking. "Boog, we gotta hide!"

But Boog was shaking all over! "I'm out of here!" he cried. Clutching his teddy bear to his chest, Boog headed to the only place that looked safe: the beaver dam.

Reilly, the head beaver, tried to stop him. "Hey! Whoa! Stop!" he yelled. "This ain't a load-bearing structure!"

It was too late, though—with Boog on the run, the dam collapsed.

A wall of water engulfed the animals and washed them away. It swept Shaw away, too! He rolled up his truck's windows and tried to speed down the dry riverbed ahead of him. But the water was rushing faster than he was, and when it roared over him, he could spot some other bodies moving in the flood. There was a beaver, some skunks, a porcupine, plus Boog and the deer!

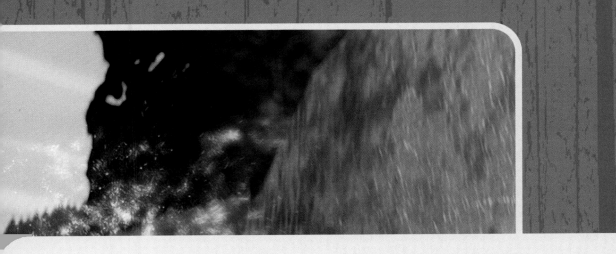

Boog and Elliot floundered in the water until Elliot pulled Boog up on a log. They paddled furiously to get away from Shaw, whose truck had surfaced like a beached whale. Then they hurtled out of the rapids into a patch of clear water . . . which suddenly gave way to a waterfall! Boog held the log and Elliot clung to his back as they sailed over it, water shooting up all around them. The animals landed on the valley floor below. Boog shook his fur dry and looked around him. Shaw was nowhere to be seen, and all the animals he'd met before were now gathered around him.

They were mad, too! "You dragged us down to the hunting grounds!" a furious Reilly shouted.

Boog wasn't about to take the blame, though, even if he was the one who'd broken the dam. Turning to Elliot, he said "If it weren't for you, I'd be home right now. You said you knew the way home—but you lied!"

He'd thought he could trust Elliot, but now he knew better: Boog could only trust himself. He didn't care what happened to Elliot or any of the other animals now. Boog stomped off from the group. He didn't know where he was going, but he was determined to find his way alone.

Boog had second thoughts during a thunderstorm, but it was too late to turn back. And then, in the distance, he could see the outline of a building—with a light on in the window! Boog bounded toward it, eager to escape the storm at last, and what he found there was beyond his wildest dreams. The place was warm and dry. There was a toilet and a refrigerator—and inside the refrigerator was a Woo-Hoo bar!

But when he turned around, Boog was in for a big surprise. The walls were covered with stuffed animal heads. And, even worse, he could hear someone turning a key in the door!

The grizzly bear shimmied up into the rafters just in time to see the door swing open . . . and Shaw strut in! "Somebody's been sitting in my chair," the hunter muttered, noticing a chair Boog had crushed. "Someone's been eating my candy. Somebody forgot to flush. And he's still here!"

Shaw's eyes darted all over the cabin, but by the time he found Boog's hiding spot, Boog had escaped to the cellar. Shaw followed him, but somehow Boog managed to flee!

In a panic, Boog ran as fast as he could, smashing through what seemed like miles of brush until he tripped and landed facedown between two yellow lines on a highway! Boog walked cautiously to the middle of the road. From there, he could see the lights of Timberline twinkling in the distance!

The bear could feel the comforts of home pulling him back. He thought of his cozy bed and his happy life with Beth. But then he thought of the heads on Shaw's wall, and knew that Elliot was in danger. He was still mad at Elliot, but he just couldn't let that happen to him. Not after all they'd been through together.

TIMBERLINE 5 mi

Boog found the animals doing their best to steer clear of the hunters. He grabbed
Elliot out of the tree where he was hiding.

"Hey, buddy," said Boog, smiling.

Elliot didn't smile back. "What are you doing here?" he asked.

"Come on," Boog said. "I couldn't go home without my partner."

It took a while to convince him, but finally Elliot decided to take Boog back.

"Okeydokey!" Elliot said with some of his old enthusiasm. "This way!" He bounded off in the wrong direction at once.

"This way," Boog declared firmly. "Let's get back to the garage, where it's *safe*!"

At that, the other animals popped out of their hiding places, too. Behind Boog and Elliot, they tiptoed toward Timberline.

"No no no no," Boog stammered when he realized what was happening. These animals couldn't possibly fit in Beth's garage!

Then he turned around and realized that was the least of his problems. The way back to town was blocked by dozens of hunters' campfires!

"I guess I *will* be mounted on a wall," moaned Elliot.

Boog looked at his frightened face, then back to the flickering fires. "No, you won't," he announced. "I ain't going out without a fight."

He thought for a moment, a plan beginning to take shape in his mind. "If there's one thing you've taught me, it's that the woods is a messed-up, dangerous place," he mused. "So I say we give our guests the full outdoor experience!"

Everyone was in, and they all cheered when Boog promised, "When we get through with them, they won't ever come back!"

Under the cover of darkness that night, the animals crept into one of the campsites. The animals took pots and pans and everything else they could find. They swiped all the food, from canned goods to marshmallows. They even stole the laundry off the clotheslines!

Suddenly they heard some furious yapping. Boog's heart sank—a little dog was going to give them away. But the dog, Mr. Weenie, drew himself up on his two hind legs and ripped off his tiny sweater. "I've been living a lie!" he confessed. "Please take me with you!" This time, Mr. Weenie didn't have to beg for anything. Boog and his friends needed all the help they could get.

At dawn, the hunters streamed from their camps through the mist, crossing a log bridge into the forest. Then they were ambushed! A team of ducks flew over the hunters, clutching skunks with their feet. When they were directly above the hunters, Rosie and Maria let it rip. They stunk out the hunters and drove them from the forest into an open meadow!

Now it was the beavers' turn. With rabbits as their gas masks, the beavers raced into the tall grass and gnawed the hunters' pants off! And then, with the hunters in shock, the deer charged through the skunk spray. It was a stampede!

Soon Boog showed up with troops of his own: squirrels, rabbits, and the porcupine. The porcupine sneezed and sprayed his quills into the hunters' skin. The rabbits pounded the hunters with spoons, forks, and knives—then Boog and Elliot squirted them with spray cheese!

The hunters knew when they were outnumbered. They painfully hobbled toward the log bridge as fast as their injuries would allow. But Reilly sawed the bridge in half, and the hunters went toppling into the water—where they were slapped around by the salmon!

Back on dry land, a dripping hunter whipped out his cell phone. "Sheriff! Sheriff!" he called. "The animals have gone wild—and the bear is their leader!"

Back in Timberline, Gordy passed his camera phone to Beth, who saw pictures of Boog's rampage. "That's it!" She gasped. "I'm bringing him home!"

Most of the hunters were retreating now, but a few die-hards stayed behind. Those remaining hunters were bombarded by squirrels carrying flaming marshmallows! Soon the last hunters were running away, afraid for their lives.

Just when Boog was feeling proud of his work, Shaw grabbed him! Elliot tried to help by smashing Shaw with the provisions they still had left: an old phone, a coffeepot, a gas can, and a pillow. It wasn't long, though, before Shaw drew his gun on the grizzly . . . and the animals didn't stand much of a chance against it.

Just as Shaw took aim at Boog, Elliot flung himself in front of his friend. Shaw's shot missed Boog—but it left Elliot crumpled in a heap on the ground.

Boog suddenly transformed into the grizzly bear of legend, a snarling and ferocious beast. The other animals were sure he was mauling Shaw. Instead, he pinned the hunter to the ground and tied him up with the barrel of his own gun! Now Shaw couldn't hurt him or anyone else if he tried.

Boog stood over Elliot's body. "You all right, Elliot?" Boog hardly dared to ask.

"Um, I'm a little light-headed," Elliot replied. His other antler fell off and hit the ground!

The other animals rushed around the grizzly and the deer, cheering and celebrating their victory over the hunters. Boog was thoughtful for a moment, gazing at the magnificent trees and the animals he'd come to know. "You know, Elliot, this place isn't so bad," he admitted.

Just then, a familiar sound echoed through the woods and a helicopter landed in the clearing. Beth emerged from the chopper, and Boog rushed to his friend, licking her from chin to forehead.

"I was so worried!" she breathed in relief. "Come on, let's go home!"

Boog would have given anything to have heard those words the day before. But now he didn't know what to do. He glanced at Elliot, and the deer stepped toward the helicopter hopefully. Boog averted his eyes to the ground and was surprised to see his teddy bear lying in the dust. He picked it up and walked toward Beth. He thought of his warm bed and the snacks Beth gave him before he went to sleep. He loved his life in Timberline . . . but he loved life in the wild, too, it turned out. And he couldn't have both.

Then the grizzly remembered what he and the animals had accomplished that morning—after that, he knew what he had to do. Boog dropped his teddy bear into Beth's hands. He looked toward the animals who were watching him from behind the trees, and she instantly understood.

"I'm gonna miss you," Beth whispered as she hugged him one last time. Boog had changed since he'd left home, and now there was no going back.

As the helicopter took off, Elliot turned to Boog, confused. "When's our pickup time?" he asked. He wasn't happy when he heard what Boog had done. "She's at least gonna bring us some Woo-Hoo bars, right?" he begged.

Boog said, "It's just the two of us, Elliot, unless you plan on going back to your herd."

"What?" yelled Elliot, smiling. "And break up the team? Bros before does!"

Just then, Giselle walked by and winked. "Hello, Elliot," she began.

Boog watched in disbelief as Elliot followed Giselle. He couldn't help but smile as he watched the scene in front of him: Reilly ran by with his chain saw, Rosie and Marie argued over one of the ducks, and Ian kept trying to walk on two legs. Boog laughed and said to himself, "Yep, feels like home, baby."